I DISAPPEAR: 3 SHORT SCREENPLAYS

by

Lee McQueen

Published by McQueen Press
http://mcqueenpress.wordpress.com

Cover image and design, interior design, typesetting by McQueen Press.

Author photo by McQueen Press.

Logo is a registered mark of McQueen Press and should not be copied without permission.

"Deep in the Woods" screenplay previously published in *The Dark Fantastic: 12 Short Screenplays* [McQueen Press, 2013].

Publisher's Catalog-in-Publication

McQueen, Lee, 1970-
I Disappear: 3 Short Screenplays/Lee McQueen
p. cm.
ISBN 978-1-7352369-0-2
    1. Motion picture plays
I. Title

WORKS BY LEE MCQUEEN

Short Story Collection

Imaginarium

Poetry Collection

Things I Forgot to Tell You

Novels

Kenzi

Celara Sun

Windrunner

The Cadis Evening

Screenplays

Kindred

SUDAN: The Lion of Truth

The Dark Fantastic: 12 Short Screenplays

Non-Fiction

Writer in the Library! 41 Writers Reveal How They Use
Libraries to Develop Their Skill, Craft & Careers

Road Romance: Tales From the Book Tour

To truly test a person's character, give that person power.

Then wait.

TABLE OF CONTENTS

INTRODUCTION

These three screenplays, "I Disappear, Alone With You Last Night, Deprivation: The Apocalypse," present an examination of the moral depths and horror that extreme income inequality and deprivation would force people to explore. In fact, the themes reflect two previous screenplays, "Deep in the Woods" (a man trades his daughter's life to save other members of his family) and "You Have to Pay the Cost to Be the Boss" (a man sells his body for medical science experimentation). Both were published 2013 in *The Dark Fantastic: 12 Short Screenplays* [McQueen Press].

I kept writing on the same speculative themes until I had five total stories that occur in the same near future universe, a North America on the brink of dystopia.

"I Disappear" is told from the perspective of a theatrical actress breaking down on stage as a result of post-traumatic stress from unknown events. "Alone With You Last Night" is somewhat lighter given the twist, however the story still reveals the predatory acts that desperation inspires. And the final warning, "Deprivation: The Apocalypse" brings it all home with the utter destruction of a society plagued by income inequality.

These three screenplays and their accompanying storyboards were actually ready for publication in 2014! I held them for six years because I felt, somehow, they went too far. Way too far. Much too far, further even than *The Dark Fantastic*. They cast unfair aspersions upon society. They were over the top. They did *way too much!*

And then, MeToo. And then, coronavirus. And then, during the first half of 2020, under the guise of this global pandemic, North America experienced a rapid and breath-taking, breath-*stealing* transfer of wealth from the lower and middle classes of millions of people to the financial elite of just a few people on an unprecedented scale. The rich got richer. The poor became poorer. Disaster capitalism. The shock doctrine.

People lost faith in political leaders, entertainers, mainstream media because of their exploitation and abuse of women and children. People lost faith in public health institutions because of contradictory and abusive political motivations in setting health policy. People rioted against unfair policing and the abuse inflicted upon citizens by law enforcement. People protested local statehouses because of lost jobs, businesses, and property due to twisted economic policies.

Suddenly, these fictional works of degradation, shame, and despair became both reality television and the evening news.

As the horror themes of the evil that men and women of power inflict on the less fortunate continued to play out in 2020, I made one last effort to combine all five short screenplays into a fictional novel that ended in a zombie apocalypse, the end goal of most dystopian societies anyway, a compliant half-dead populace. In this way, I could pretend it wasn't real, that it wasn't really happening. It was just my imagination, a nightmare. But I just couldn't make it work because real life kept intruding. Once again, I felt that small doses of fiction would be easier to digest, at least for me, in light of what was already happening in the real world.

And so, after much procrastination, delay, and "over-thinking," I hereby release *I Disappear: 3 Short Screenplays* into the universe to serve as a reflection, if no longer a prediction and a warning, of a nation on the brink of decline.

It is my sincere hope that the world rights itself, and that people are allowed to live good lives and to become better citizens and neighbors and friends to each other. I'm quite convinced that the world is a much better place to live in when many are happy instead of just a few.

Lee McQueen, July 2020

Screenplay 1

I DISAPPEAR

Cast of Characters

Tamerlane – Black female, 30s

State manager – Male, 40s, any race

Cashier/Usher – Female, 20s, any race

FADE IN:

EXT. THEATER – LATE AFTERNOON

A small theater has "'I Disappear,' a one-woman, one-act special engagement starring Tamerlane," on the marquee.

INT. THEATER: STAGE – LATE AFTERNOON

Tamerlane stands in a spotlight.

She turns her back to the camera.

                    TAMERLANE
          Don't hide from what your are, when
          you are the same.

                    STAGE MANAGER
          Cue lights.

The lights in the theater go dark.

                    STAGE MANAGER (in earpiece)
          Cue lights and fog machine. Cue
          Tamerlane.

The lights come back on. Fog surrounds Tamerlane.

                    STAGE MANAGER
          Turn back to the audience. Fade to back
          and exit stage right.

Tamerlane disappears.

                    STAGE MANAGER (in earpiece)
          Cue lights.

The stage lights go dark.

> STAGE MANAGER
> Cue Tamerlane. Return for bow.

Tamerlane re-enters the stage and takes a bow.

The Stage Manager, Lighting Technician, and Cashier/Usher applaud.

> STAGE MANAGER
> Excellent work, Tamerlane. Reset, everyone. Forty minutes to showtime.

Tamerlane smiles and walks off stage.

She pauses by the fog machine.

The fog machine sits silent, as if waiting for something to happen.

INT. THEATER:LOBBY - NIGHT

Hands tear the bottom of an invitation.

> CASHIER/USHER (voice only)
> Short play tonight, folks. No intermission. Make sure to stay until the very end for the door prize.

"I Disappear" stubs pile into a basket.

Hands grab at complimentary glasses of wine and treats.

INT. THEATER:DRESSING ROOM – NIGHT

Tamerlane stares into a mirror.

But what she's looking at is a small photo of a little girl tucked into the mirror's frame.

Tamerlane covers her face with her hands, as the child in the photo looks on.

Tamerlane removes her hands and recovers her nerve with a steely smile.

INT. THEATER:STAGE – NIGHT

Voices of a full house quiet when the Stage Manager walks on and holds up his hands.

> STAGE MANAGER
> Thank you, everyone for coming out for this exclusive, invitation-only showing of I Disappear, starring Tamerlane. Only certain members of the community received this invitation for the special preview of Tamerlane's one-act, one-woman play. Those of us who regularly work with children understand how important they are and how funding resources often do not match their needs. Proceeds from tonight's show will be awarded to the door prize winner along with a matching grant from our hometown girl made good, Tamerlane.

The audience applauds and whistles.

> STAGE MANAGER
> Well, in my book, those who work in defense of children are all winners.

Applause.

STAGE MANAGER
And now, ladies and gentlemen, and everyone else...

Laughter from the audience.

STAGE MANAGER
Tamerlane!

The curtain moves back.

Tamerlane stands in spotlight in a really weird, exotic, dangerously beautiful costume.

She moves gracefully about the stage, owning the space, displaying years of disciplined dance training.

She stands still, looking at the audience.

TAMERLANE
Wild Hazy stormed into my life
Brassy sassy racy spacey frenzied pepper spice
Brilliantly flashed, she flamed with no shame
Clashed and smashed, then claimed the pain
You left when the storm, the torrent that formed
Came and hurricaned your dreams away

Tamerlane walks into the audience and winds her way through the aisles.

TAMERLANE
Beautiful Crazy, she surprised them all
Shocked and rocked but stopped right before the fall
Cruel and angry to defend, scorched but free
Driven by the wind and gripped a piercing breeze

She soared and seared and danced, such grace
Loved, but truly feared, debased and erased

Tamerlane stands once again on stage.

> TAMERLANE
> Don't any of you remember me?

> STAGE MANAGER (in earpiece)
> Is she off script? Where is she?
> Tamerlane?

> TAMERLANE
> Pretty Lady...

> STAGE MANAGER (in earpiece)
> Okay, we're back.

> TAMERLANE
> Floating the carousel
> That cool attitude in this rough world
> Chemical miracle to give you the best in
> dreams

Cut to:

INT. THEATER:LOBBY – NIGHT

Dozens of empty wine glasses surround empty wine bottles.

INT. THEATER:STAGE – NIGHT

> TAMERLANE
> Still, in spite of it all, you shine, you
> sheen

> Take me where you are, far away from here
> Far away from me, I long for the serene

                    STAGE MANAGER
          It's beautiful, Tamerlane. Beautiful.

Tamerlane's movements around the stage become more intense.

                    TAMERLANE
          Definitely Maybe, cannot handle you
          Baby

Cut to:

INT. THEATER:DRESSING ROOM – NIGHT

The picture of the little girl still looks on Tamerlane's dressing room.

INT. THEATER:STAGE – NIGHT

                    TAMERLANE
          You stay just to say but you want to play free
          You know what they see, what they think when asleep
          For you, only you, they allow you to peek

                    STAGE MANAGER (in earpiece)
          Prepare for light cue.

                    TAMERLANE
          Fighting a system that kidnaps your name

Tamerlane turns her back

                    TAMERLANE
          Don't fight what you are, when you are
          the same

                    STAGE MANAGER (in earpiece)
          Cue lights.

The lights go dark.

                    STAGE MANAGER (in earpiece)
          Cue lights and fog machine. Cue
          Tamerlane for turn.

Still masked, Tamerlane turns surrounded by fogged lights.

                    STAGE MANAGER (in earpiece)
          Cue Tamerlane, exit stage right.

Tamerlane doesn't move.

                    STAGE MANAGER
          Tamerlane, exit stage right.

Tamerlane doesn't move. No sound from the audience.

                    STAGE MANAGER (in earpiece)
          Tamerlane, we just did this in rehearsal.
          What are... That's not your costume.
          Why... why are you wearing a gas mask?

Tamerlane doesn't respond. The audience doesn't applaud.

A long, awkward moment passes.

STAGE MANAGER

Oh my God. Greg! Turn off the fog machine. Turn it off! Stop the fogger! Tamerlane (long pause) what have you done? Sheila!

Tamerlane darts from the stage.

STAGE MANAGER (in earpiece)

Sheila! Open the house doors. Open the doors! Please, oh my God! Sheila! Sheila!

INT. THEATER:DRESSING ROOM – NIGHT

Tamerlane flies into the doorway of the dressing room like a bird of prey.

INT. THEATER:STAGE – NIGHT

The Stage Manager crawls to open the house doors.

STAGE MANAGER

Why, Tamerlane? Why?

His hand slides from the door handles and he chokes out on the floor.

INT. THEATER:BACKSTAGE – NIGHT

The camera sweeps the audience, all dead, then the Stage Manager, also dead.

The camera whirls back stage to Tamerlane's dressing room. The photo of the young girl has been altered with a mask drawn on that resembles Tamerlane's mask.

The camera whirls and follows Tamerlane's escape path through the back door.

Tamerlane's footsteps and shadow lead the camera down the alley behind the theater.

The camera races past her discarded costume.

Tamerlane runs through moonlight, then disappears into shadow.

FADE OUT
THE END

Storyboards

I DISAPPEAR

I DISAPPEAR

Storyboard Title Card

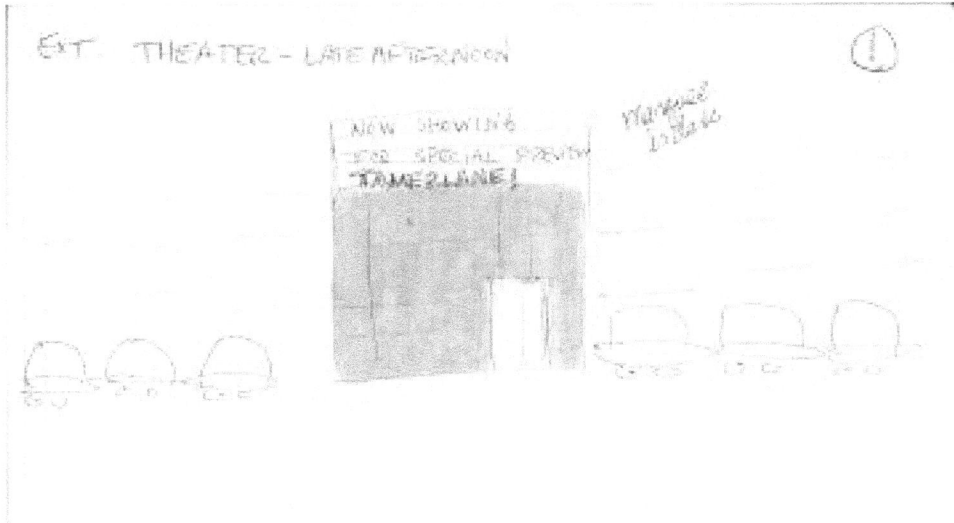

Storyboard 1

Storyboard 2

Storyboard 3

Storyboard 4

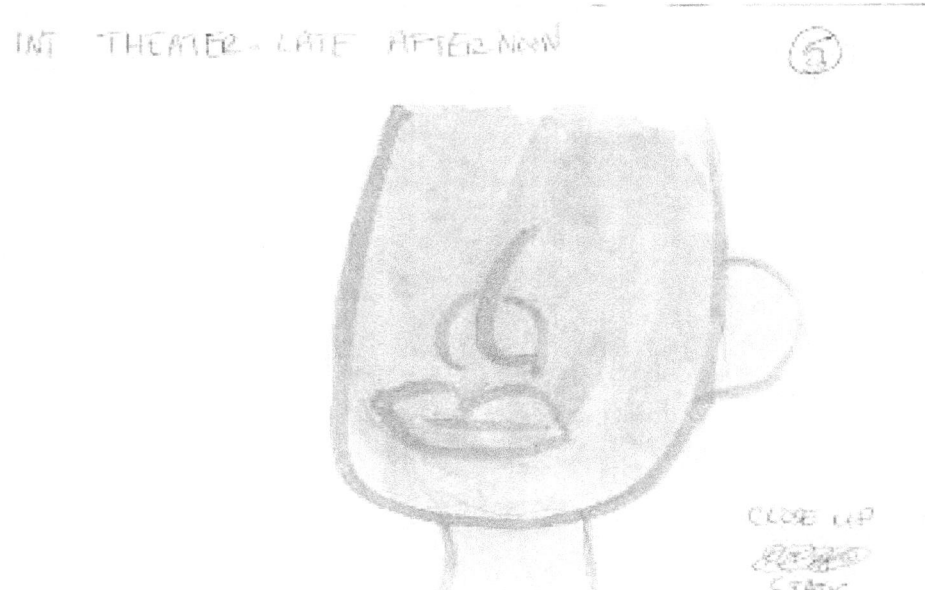

Storyboard 5

Storyboard 6

Storyboard 7

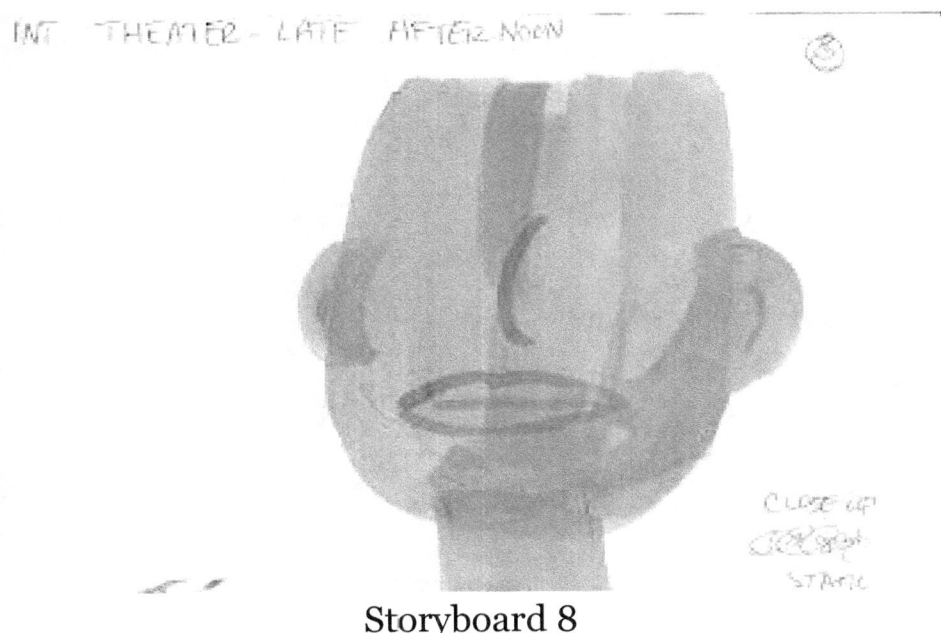

Storyboard 8

Storyboard 9

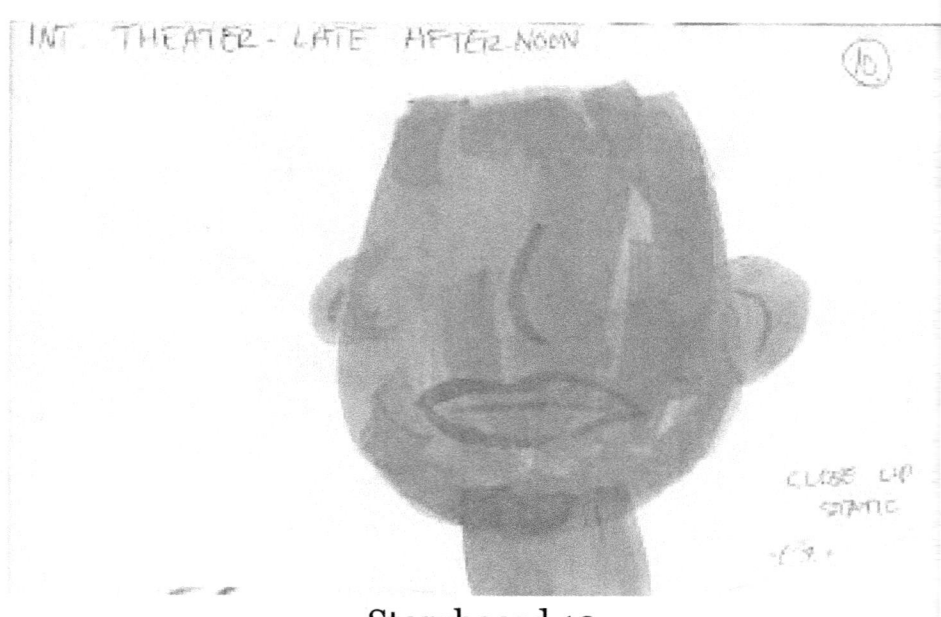

INT. THEATER - LATE AFTERNOON ⑩

CLOSE UP
STATIC

Storyboard 10

INT. THEATER. BACK-STAGE - LATE AFTERNOON ⑪

Back shot
upward

Pan down

MEDIUM
HAND HELD

Storyboard 11

INT THEATER BACKSTAGE - LATE AFTERNOON (12)

FOG MACHINE

MEDIUM
HAND HELD

Storyboard 12

INT THEATER BACKSTAGE - LATE AFTERNOON (12.1)

STATIC

Storyboard 12.1

Storyboard 13

Storyboard 14

MEDIUM

CRITIC

Sound: Tibton Jabber of Crowd

Storyboard 15

INT. THEATER - DUSK ⑯

Sound Tibton Jabber/laughter of Crowd   MEDIUM   CRITIC

Storyboard 16

Storyboard 17

Storyboard 18

Storyboard 19

Storyboard 20

Storyboard 21

Storyboard 22

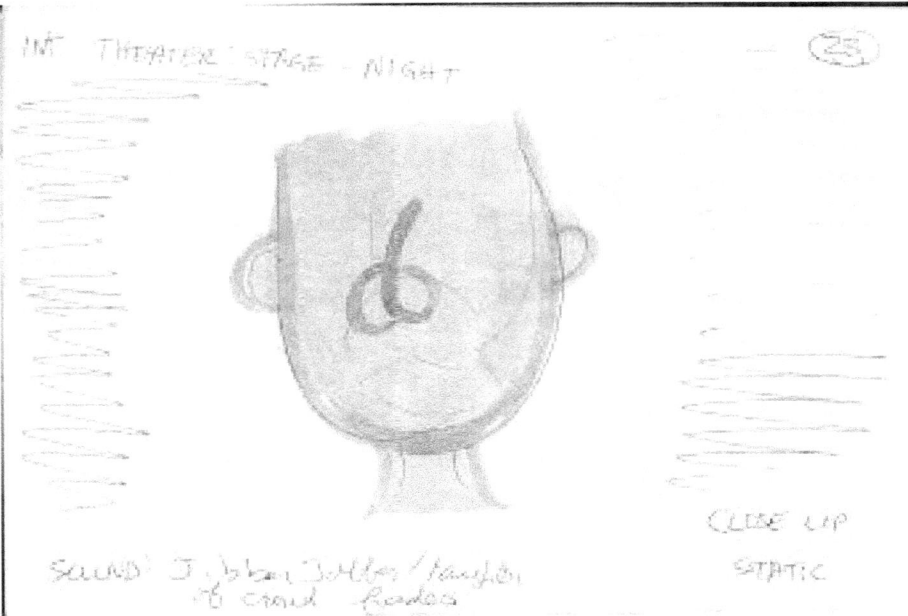

Storyboard 23

Storyboard 24

Storyboard 25

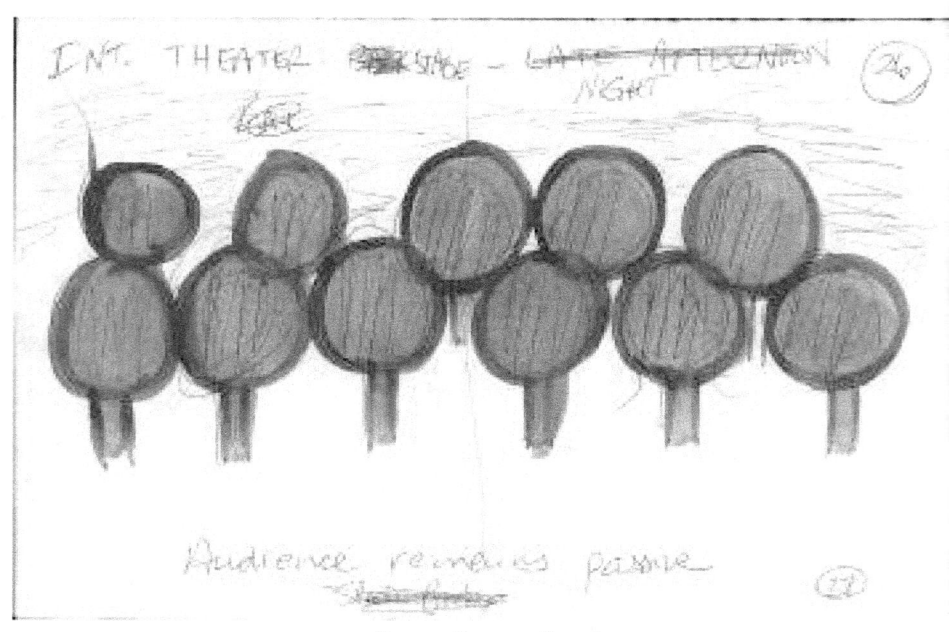

Storyboard 26

Storyboard 27

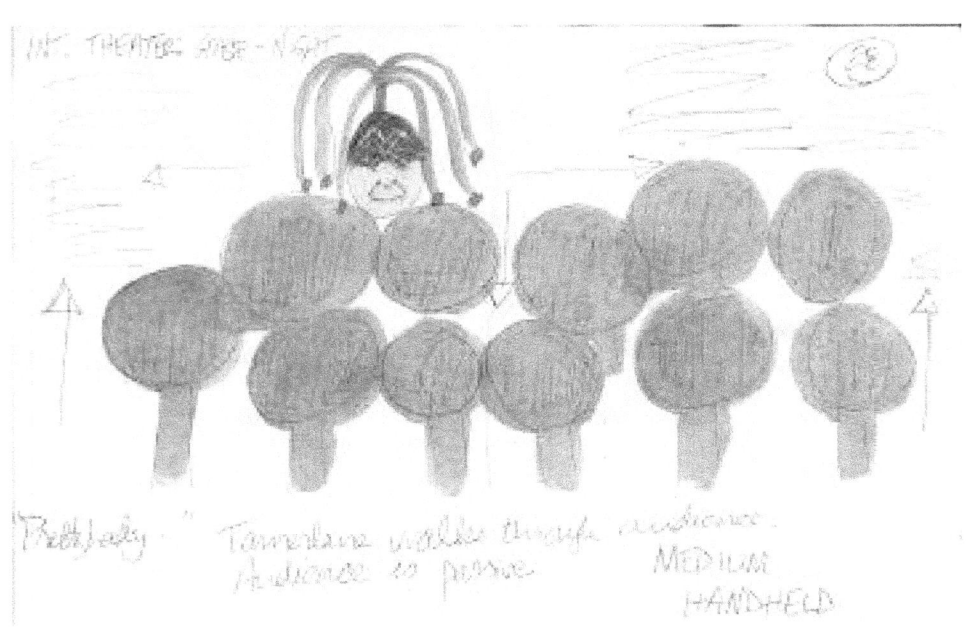

Storyboard 28

Storyboard 29

Storyboard 30

28 LEE MCQUEEN

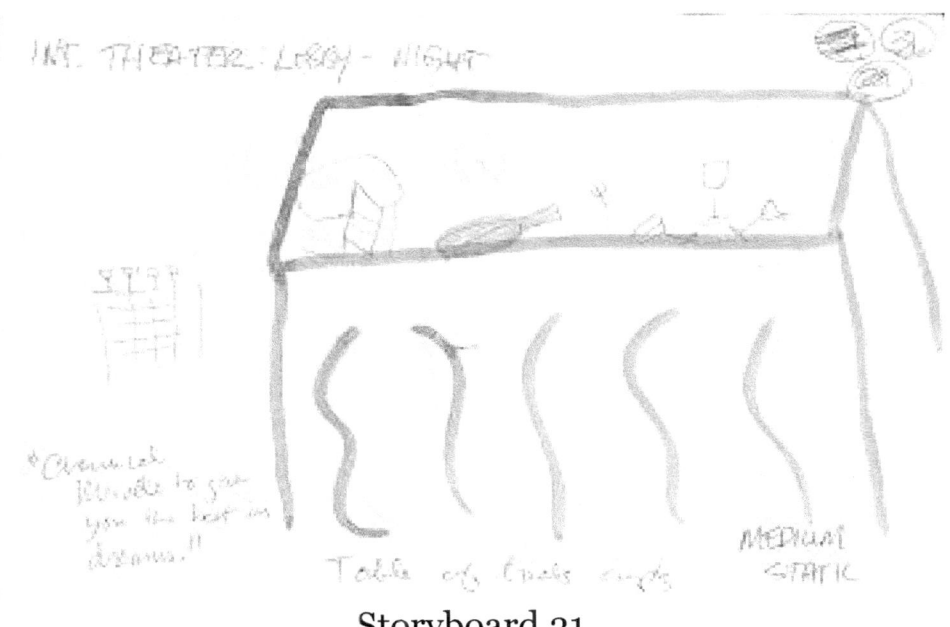

Storyboard 31

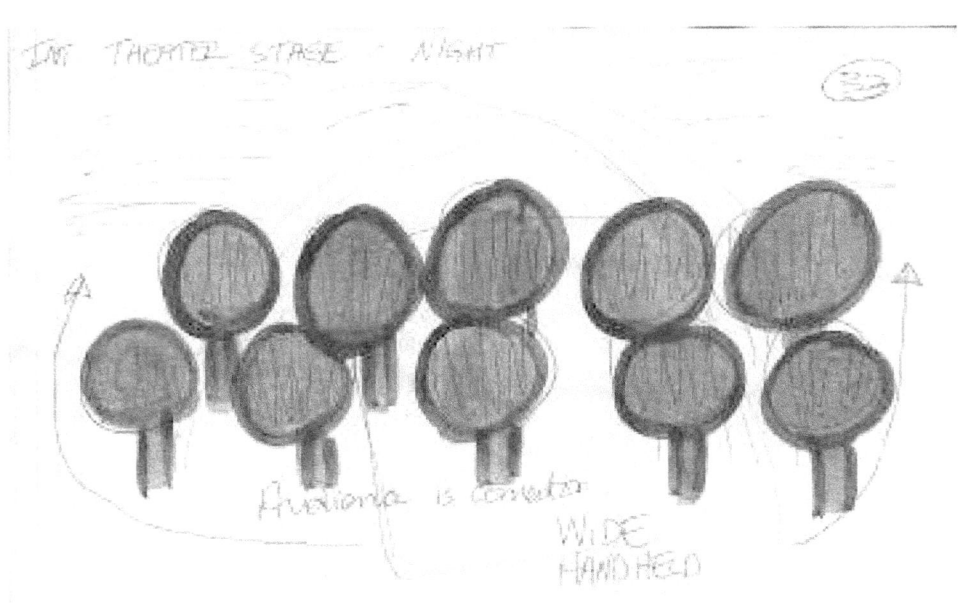

Storyboard 32

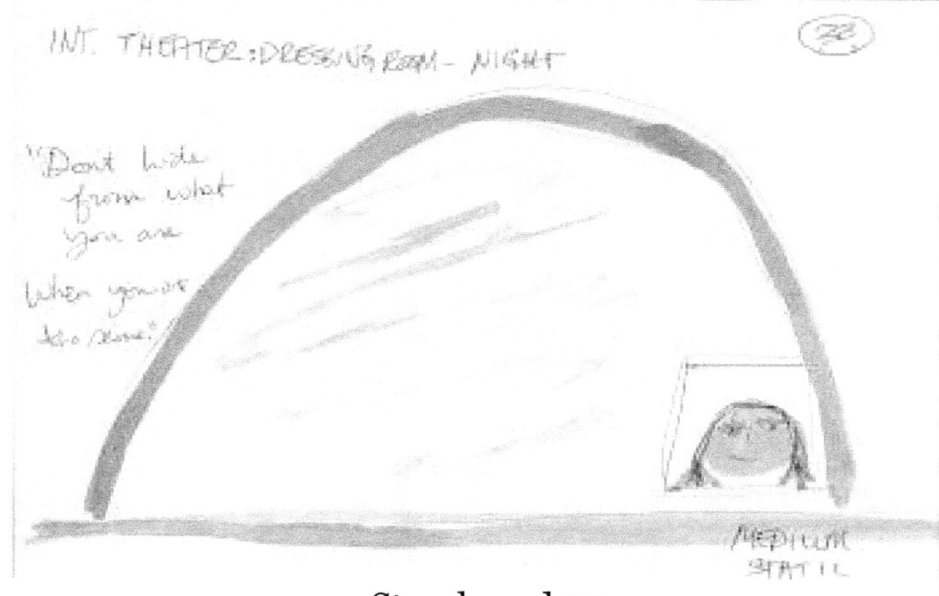

Storyboard 33

Storyboard 34

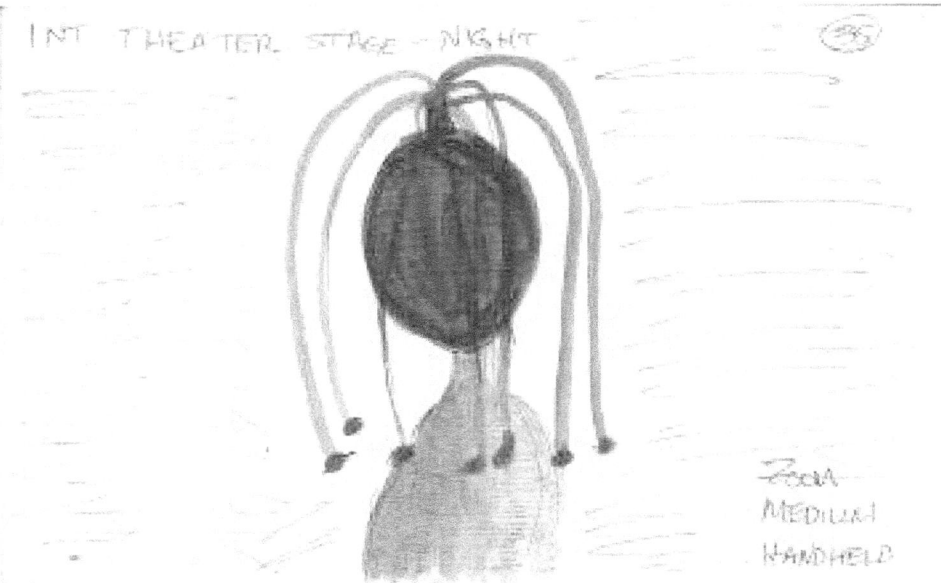

INT THEATER STAGE - NIGHT

35

ZOOM
MEDIUM
HANDHELD

Storyboard 35

INT THEATER BACKSTAGE - NIGHT

36

FOG
MACHINE

MEDIUM
STATIC

Storyboard 36

Storyboard 37

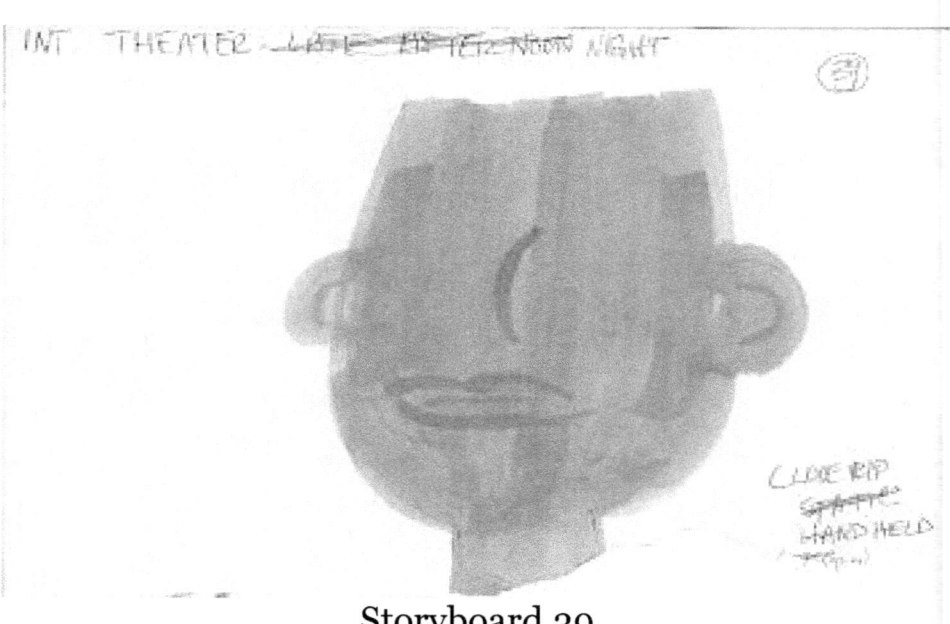

Storyboard 39

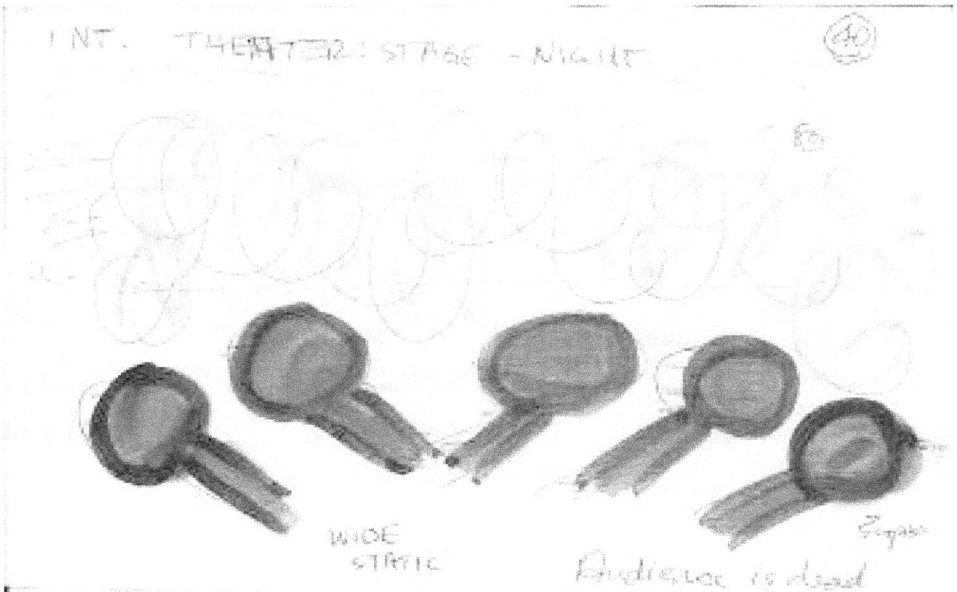

INT. THEATER: STAGE - NIGHT (40)

WIDE
STATIC

Audience is dead

Storyboard 40

INT. THEATER: BACK STAGE - NIGHT (41)

Gray Static!

CLOSE UP
HANDHELD

Storyboard 41

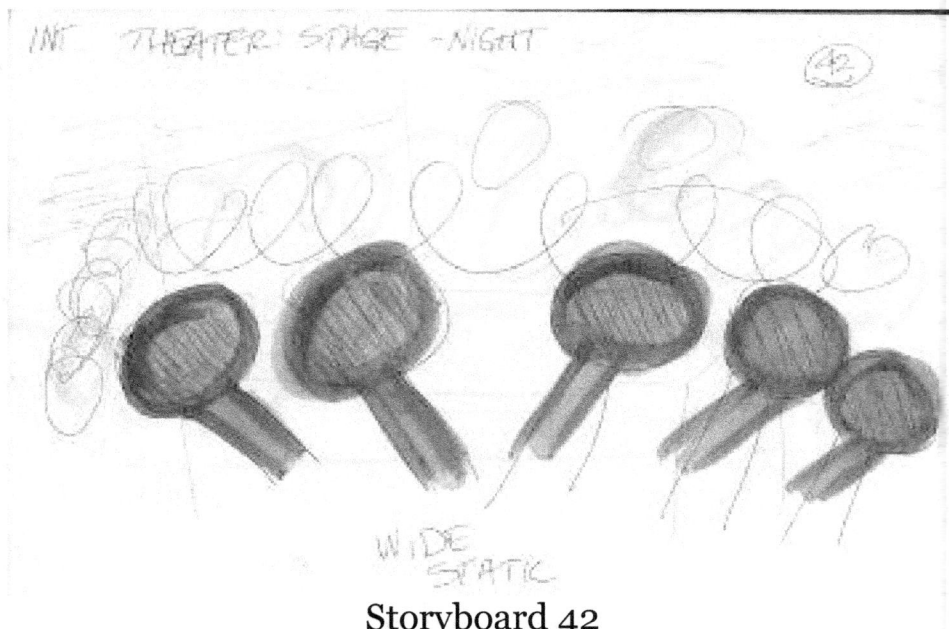

Storyboard 42

Storyboard 43

Storyboard 44

Storyboard 45

Storyboard 46

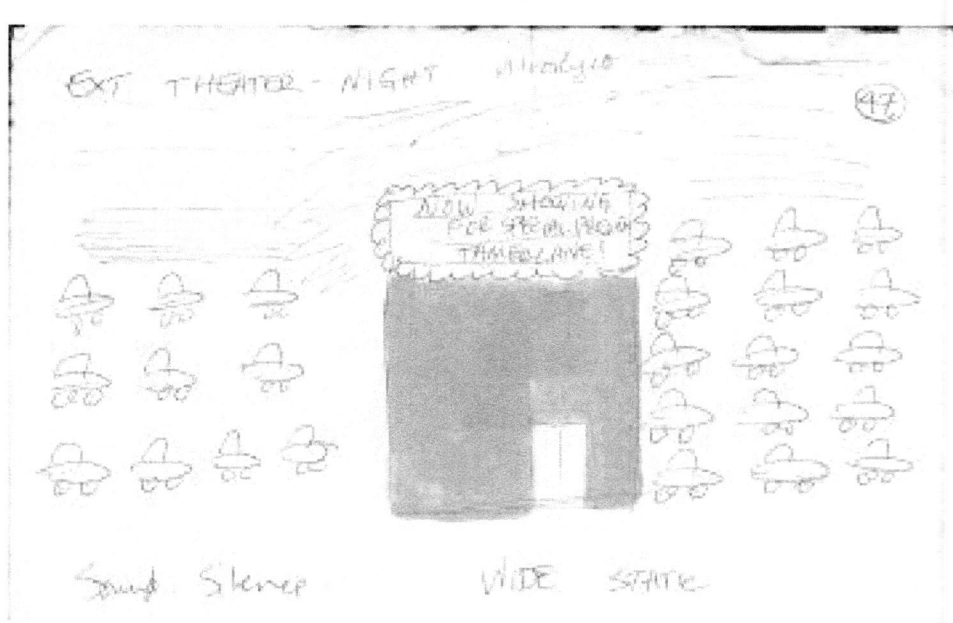

Storyboard 47

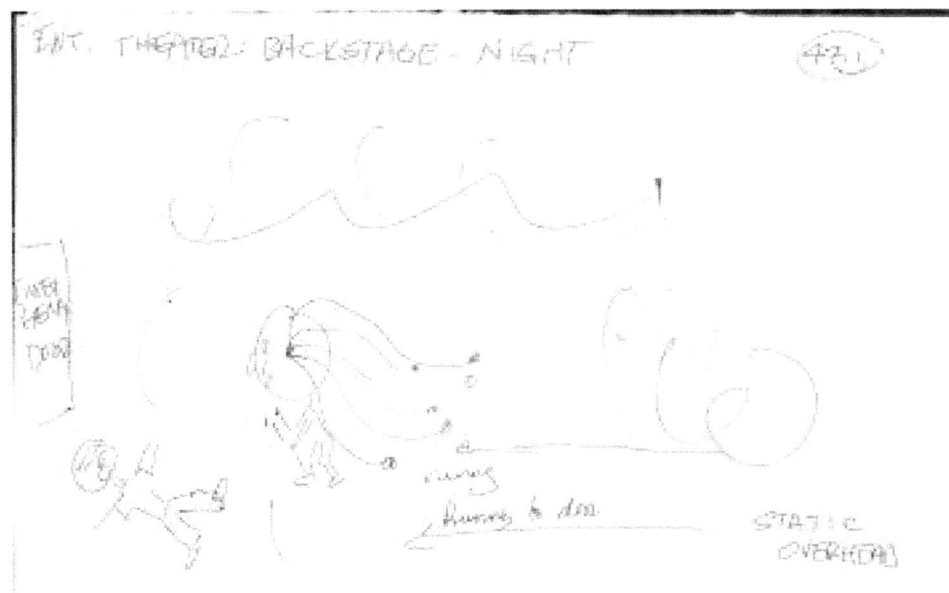

Storyboard 47.1

Storyboard 48

Storyboard 49

Storyboard 50

Storyboard 51

Storyboard 53

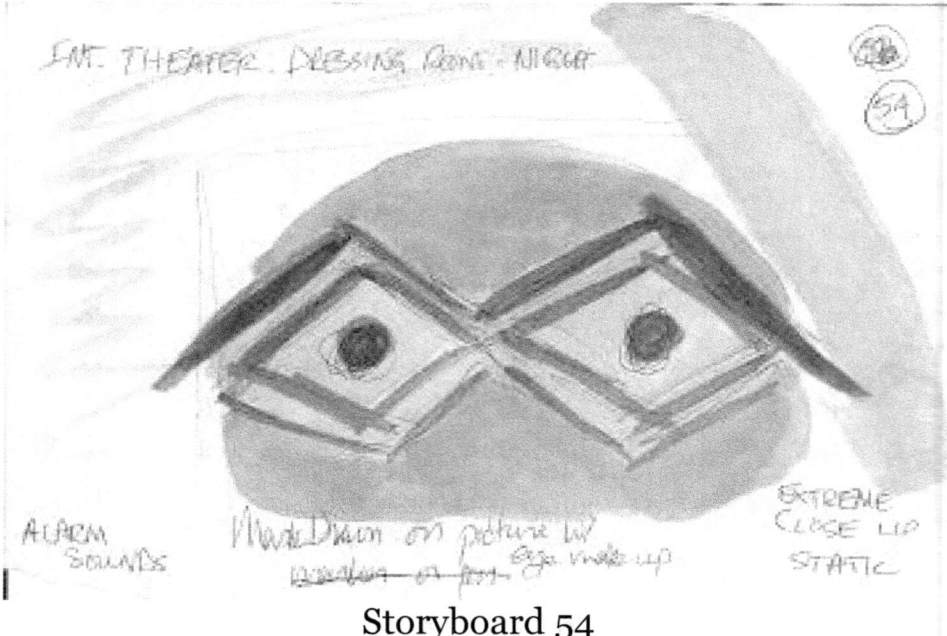

INT. THEATER. DRESSING ROOM - NIGHT

ALARM SOUNDS

MoveDown on picture w/ ~~picture~~ of face eye make up

EXTREME CLOSE UP STATIC

Storyboard 54

EXT. THEATER ALLEY - NIGHT

ALARM SOUNDS

CLOSE UP STATIC

Storyboard 56

Storyboard 57

Storyboard 58

I DISAPPEAR

Storyboard End Card

Screenplay 2

ALONE WITH YOU LAST NIGHT

CAST OF CHARACTERS

WOMAN – 25-45-years-old, Black, Female

MAN – 25-45-years-old, any race/ethnicity, Male

TRAIN OPERATOR – any age, race, ethnicity, gender

FADE IN

EXT./INT. TRAIN CAR – NIGHT

At 3:00am, an inebriated, well-dressed WOMAN with an expensive leather purse stumbles into a subway car at the Lake stop and falls into a seat.

She turns and waves, giggling.

> WOMAN
> See you guys! No. Sleep. Till Bryn Mawr!

The train doors shut and the train rumbles along the track.

INT. TRAIN CAR – NIGHT

Still smiling, the Woman's eyes flicker.

Mechanical noise like gears, doors, and destination announcements fill a minute-long silence.

Still smiling, the Woman's head nods forward then back.

She's asleep by the time the train car passes through the Chicago stop.

The camera finds a casually-dressed MAN at the other end of the car eyeing the Woman.

EXT./INT. TRAIN CAR – NIGHT

The train roars through tunnels. Lights in the tunnel stream and flicker with a strobe effect.

Suddenly, the Man is standing in front of the Woman.

He crouches in front of her, not looking at her face, but at her abdomen.

He pulls out a knife that glints in the strobe lights and draws his arm back. The Man's arm saws back and forth.

The woman's head wobbles with the movement of the train car, but jerks at least once from the man's intense knife work.

The Man puts the knife back into his pocket.

INT. TRAIN CAR – NIGHT

He uses his hands to tear.

There is a sound of ripping skin.

The Man smiles greedily.

He begins extraction.

The Woman is still passed out, but her face twitches and her breathing changes.

The man stands and backs away, satisfied.

EXT./INT. TRAIN CAR – NIGHT

A computerized voices announces, "This is Bryn Mawr."

The man waits for the subway doors to open, then exits.

The voice announces, "The next stop is Thorndale. Doors open on the left at Thorndale."

INT. TRAIN CAR – NIGHT

The Woman's eyes snap open.

She stares at the train car ceiling.

She raises her head and looks around to find herself very alone.

The train car shudders and jerks and begins to pull away from the Bryn Mawr station.

The Woman sits up. She senses something's very wrong.

She looks down and then starts screaming.

> WOMAN
> Nooooo! Nooooo! Nooooo! Nooooo! Nooooo!

She crawls to the emergency call button and pounds it, crying hysterically.

> TRAIN OPERATOR (voice)
> Is there an emergency? Do you need help?

> WOMAN
> Help me! Please help me!

The train car jerks to a stop. The doors open and close.

> TRAIN OPERATOR (voice)
> What kind of help do you require, ma'am?

> WOMAN
> I... I... He cut while I was asleep. He used a knife on me. He took them. He took everything! God help me!

> TRAIN OPERATOR (voice)
> Ma'am, I'm on my way to your car.
> Police in the area have been notified.
> I've locked the doors. Stay in the car!

An announcement over the sound system... "We are paused momentarily due to a problem with the train's operation. The conductor and other train personnel are working to resolve this issue."

The Woman weeps and slides to a prone position on the train floor.

> WOMAN (whispering)
> Help me. Help me.

EXT./INT. TRAIN CAR – NIGHT

The Train Conductor looks through the emergency door of another car and shouts to the Woman, who doesn't respond.

The Train Conductor opens the train doors.

> TRAIN CONDUCTOR
> Ma'am. Oh my God! What did he do to
> you?

EXT. STREET – NIGHT

The Man whistles a happy tune.

EXT./INT. TRAIN CAR – NIGHT

The Train Conductor turns the Woman over and sees...

An expensive leather purse with a big hole in the side emptied of everything valuable.

EXT. STREET – NIGHT

The Man counts cash and sorts through credit cards like a croupier with a deck of cards.

Then he snaps a cheerful selfie with the woman's cell phone.
EXT./INT. TRAIN CAR – NIGHT

The Woman screams in prolonged anguish that echoes across a dark cityscape.

EXT. STREET – NIGHT

The Man half-turns to listen.

Then he boards a passing bus.

FADE OUT
THE END

Storyboards

ALONE WITH YOU LAST NIGHT

50 LEE MCQUEEN

Storyboard Title Card

Storyboard 1

Storyboard 1.2

Storyboard 1.3

Storyboard 2

Storyboard 2.3

Storyboard 2.4

Storyboard 3

Storyboard 4

Storyboard 5

Storyboard 6

Storyboard 7

Storyboard 8

Storyboard 9

Storyboard 10

Storyboard 11

Storyboard 11.1

Storyboard 12

Storyboard 13

Storyboard 14

Storyboard 15

Storyboard 16

Storyboard 17

Storyboard 17.1

Storyboard 18

Storyboard 19

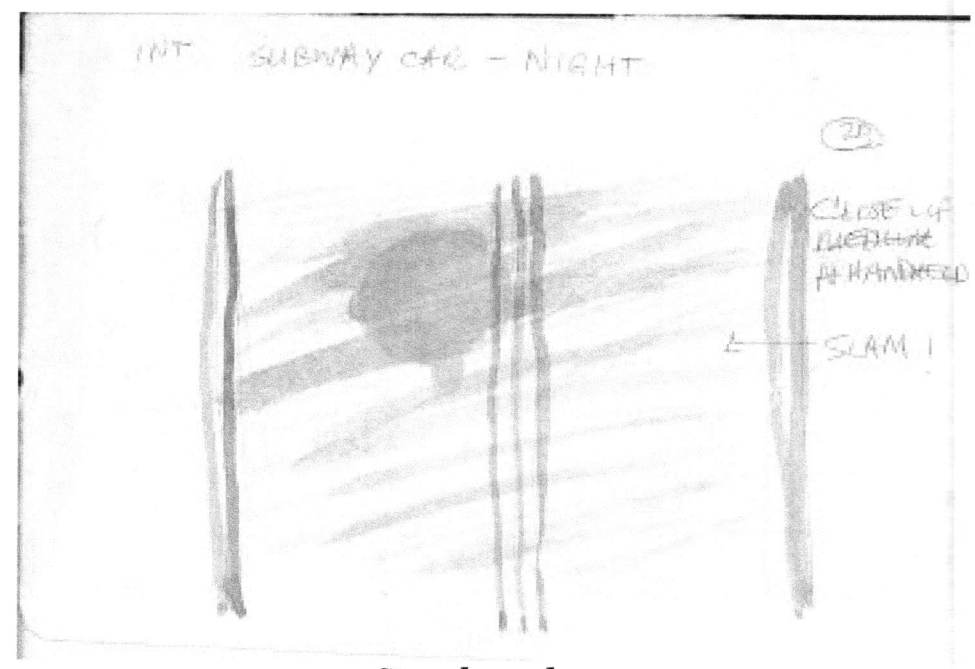

Storyboard 20

Storyboard 21

Storyboard 21.1

Storyboard 22

Storyboard 23

Storyboard 24

Storyboard 25

Storyboard 26

Storyboard 27

Storyboard 28

Storyboard 29

Storyboard 29.1

Storyboard 29.2

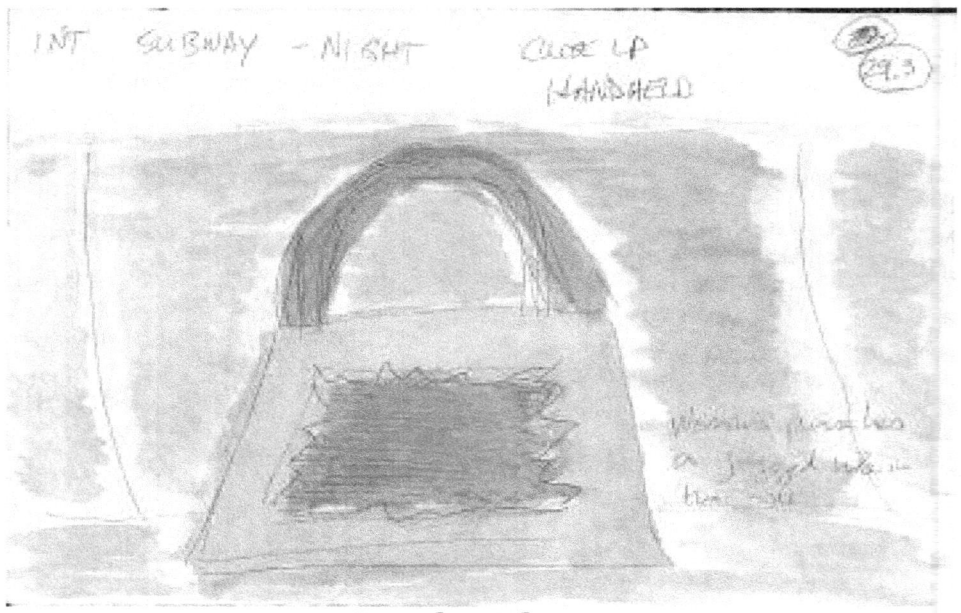

Storyboard 29.3

Storyboard 30

Storyboard 31

Storyboard 33

Storyboard 32

Storyboard 35

Storyboard End Card

Screenplay 3

DEPRIVATION: THE APOCALYPSE

CAST OF CHARACTERS

HOMELESS WOMAN – 25-45-years-old, Black, Female

POLICE OFFICER – 20-65-years-old, any race, Male or Female

SECURITY GUARD – 20-65-years-old, any race, Male or Female

BUSINESS OWNER – 20-65-years-old, any race, Male or Female

HOUSED RESIDENT – 20-65-years-old, any race, Male or Female

HOMELESS EXTRAS – 20-80-years-old, all
races/ethnicities/genders

FADE IN

EXT./INT. BUILDING – DAY

Moaning and groaning HOMELESS EXTRAS break windows and doors amid screams and shouts.

Title Card:
We already walk among you.

INT. PUBLIC LIBRARY - DAY

A SECURITY GUARD crosses his arms.

                    SECURITY GUARD
          You can't sleep here, miss.

INT. METRA TRAIN STATION:LOBBY - DAY

A POLICE OFFICER stands arms akimbo.

                    POLICE OFFICER
          You got to go *now*.

INT. FAST FOOD RESTAURANT - NIGHT

A BUSINESS OWNER taps on the table.

                    BUSINESS OWNER
          Wake up, lady.

INT. GROCERY STORE:BATHROOM – DAY

Door opens. Security Guard stands in the doorway.

HOMELESS WOMAN turns from mirror holding a toothbrush.

>   SECURITY GUARD (shaking
>   head)
> No, miss. No. That's not gonna work.

>   HOMELESS WOMAN
> I'm almost done, I was just...

>   SECURITY GUARD
> About to do that at your own house.

>   HOMELESS WOMAN
> You'd think people would have more of
> an issue if I *didn't* brush my teeth than if
> I did.

>   SECURITY GUARD
> Don't mess up this bathroom for others.

>   HOMELESS WOMAN
> Mess up... I lost my job, not my
> humanity. I'm still a human being.

>   SECURITY GUARD
> Move *along*, please.

Homeless Woman puts away her toothbrush.

INT. METRA TRAIN STATION:LOBBY - DAY

Homeless Woman sits on bench with a book.

HOMELESS WOMAN
I'm just tired that's all.

POLICE OFFICER
Ma'am, are we going to have a problem?

Homeless Woman shakes her head, closes book, and rises.

HOMELESS WOMAN
No. I was just sitting.

POLICE OFFICER
Not anymore. Move along.

INT. FAST FOOD RESTAURANT – NIGHT

Homeless Woman sits at a table with empty food wrappers.

HOMELESS WOMAN
I bought a sandwich. See? I have the
receipt right here.

BUSINESS OWNER
You ate the sandwich. Sandwich is gone.
No more sandwich here.

HOMELESS WOMAN
Look, I'm not crazy or dangerous.
I'm low-income.

BUSINESS OWNER
Sandwich go bye-bye half hour ago. You
are no longer a customer. You go bye-
bye too. Bye-bye!

Homeless Woman clears the table.

EXT. METRA TRAIN STATION:LOBBY - DAY

Homeless Woman walks slowly towards the exit followed closely by the Police Officer.

> HOMELESS WOMAN
> Poverty seems like some kind of felony lately.

> POLICE OFFICER
> If you would please continue forward motion, ma'am. Thank you.

INT. COLLEGE:LOBBY - DAY

Homeless Woman puts down her pencil and looks up.

> SECURITY GUARD
> You can't hang out here because then the whole community will want to hang out here.

> HOMELESS WOMAN
> The community is already hanging out here. It's a *community* college.

Security Guard points to the door.

Homeless Woman sighs and rises to her feet.

INT. METRA TRAIN STATION:LOBBY - DAY

Homeless Woman slows down to rest next to the front entrance.

                    POLICE OFFICER
You've got ten minutes to pack it up and
move it along.

                    WOMAN
You're acting like I ran over and
snatched the doughnut out of your hand.
Why are you hassling me so hard?

                    POLICE OFFICER
In ten minutes, you're gonna be a
problem for me to solve. Got it?

Homeless Woman nods, with weary humiliation.

EXT. APARTMENT BUILDING:LANDSCAPE - NIGHT

Homeless Woman sits in a gazebo covered by a blanket.

                    HOUSED RESIDENT
You can't sleep out here, lady. This is
our home. *Our* home. Not yours!

                    HOMELESS WOMAN
I'm sorry. I'll just get my things together
and go.

                    HOUSED RESIDENT
We pay rent!

INT. MUSEUM - DAY

                    SECURITY GUARD (shouting)
Eyes open!

INT. SHOPPING MALL - NIGHT

> POLICE OFFICER (shouting)
> Get up!

INT. FAST FOOD RESTAURANT - NIGHT

> BUSINESS OWNER (shouting)
> Wake up and get up. Then shut up and
> get out!

EXT. APARTMENT BUILDING:LANDSCAPE - NIGHT

> HOUSED RESIDENT (shouting)
> I've already called the police. They're
> coming right now. They know what you
> look like!

INT. CATHOLIC CHURCH – DAY

In the last row of benches, Homeless Woman's head nods and jerks.

> SECURITY GUARD
> You need to go. This place is for the
> worshipful.

> HOMELESS WOMAN
> I'm a Christian.

> SECURITY GUARD
> I saw you. You were not worshiping.

> HOMELESS WOMAN
> I was actually meditating.

SECURITY GUARD
You were actually sleeping.

Long pause.

HOMELESS WOMAN
It's below freezing outside.

Security Guard points to the door.

EXT. PARK:BENCH – DAY

Homeless Woman sits on a park bench wrapped in a blanket, shivering.

She speaks directly to the camera.

HOMELESS WOMAN
I mean, I've tried sleeping rough and I
don't recommend it. I woke up with feet
like blocks of ice. Like frozen bricks.

Homeless Woman stands and shuffles slowly away from the bench.

INT./EXT. FAST FOOD RESTAURANT – DAY

Homeless Woman stands in doorway facing the scowling Business Owner.

HOMELESS WOMAN
I can't feel my feet.

The Business Owner's face softens.

Homeless Woman enters the restaurant and speaks to the camera.

> HOMELESS WOMAN
> I warm myself in this fine establishment
> for the ten minutes that I'm allowed. I
> say a prayer of thanks that I wake up in
> time not to lose toes to frost bite. So
> basically, it's mostly a good night. Sort
> of.

Homeless Woman tries and fails to smile.

EXT. EL TRAIN STATION:LOBBY – DAY

Homeless Woman speaks to the camera.

> HOMELESS WOMAN
> Survival mode. Well, game on. I *have* to
> stay alive. I won't go gently into that
> good night. I just won't do it.

INT. SOUP KITCHEN – NIGHT

Homeless Woman holds a plate of rice.

> HOMELESS WOMAN
> Just the rice for me. I'm a vegetarian, so
> I'll leave the meat and gravy for the
> others.

Rough hands snatch the plate from Homeless Woman and
slap meat and gravy all over the rice.

Fingers point to a sign on the wall, "All guests eat the plate
that you're given!"

Homeless Woman sits and hands her plate to the person
beside her then turns to the camera.

> HOMELESS WOMAN
> I have to do whatever it takes to survive, within reason. I don't want to go to jail. Although I hear it's warm there. And they have food. And maybe they'd let me sleep through the night...

INT. DAY SHELTER:DESK – DAY

Low voices murmur together while Homeless Woman stands waiting for recognition.

Finally...

> HOMELESS WOMAN
> Hi there! I'd like to sign up to do laundry today, if I could.

The low voices continue murmuring.

> HOMELESS WOMAN
> Excuse me. Hate to interrupt, but is a washing machine available?

Muted laughter.

> HOMELESS WOMAN
> I... have my clothes ready to go right here, if it's okay.

> OFF-CAMERA VOICE
> Just a minute! I'll be with you in a second, if you can be patient. Jeez!

Low voices continue murmuring.

Homeless Woman waits a moment, then turns to the camera and opens her mouth as if to speak.

> OFF-CAMERA VOICE
> Okay, miss. What do you want *this* time?
> What's so important?

Homeless Woman smiles at the camera.

> HOMELESS WOMAN
> I apologize in advance to the entire city
> on whose nerves I'm about to *really* get.

EXT. EL TRAIN STATION:LOBBY – NIGHT

Homeless Woman turns stares at the empty gate attendant's booth.

> HOMELESS WOMAN
> No gate attendant because he's asleep.
> Or he took off work early. Or he's in the
> bathroom. (at camera) No problem.

INT. ART GALLERY – NIGHT

Homeless Woman holds a plate of food and a cup of wine.

She stares at a bizarre art piece and tilts her head.

> HOMELESS WOMAN
> Free reception on opening night. The art
> gallery doesn't mind because I mingle
> and mix well with the crowd.

Homeless Woman laughs and jabbers complete nonsense.

INT. MOVIE THEATER – NIGHT

Homeless Woman sits in a chair in the dark and speaks to the movie screen.

> HOMELESS WOMAN
> Free advance screening. No wake up calls from the movie usher because it's dark and, face it, (whispers to camera) I'm not the only one sleeping here.

Wide-eyed, homeless Woman covers her mouth with her hand.

INT. BUSINESS CONFERENCE – DAY

Homeless Woman fills a plate with muffins and pours coffee.

She fills her pockets with extra butter and sugar packets.

> HOMELESS WOMAN
> Free employment and business networking. I happen to own a suit. I'm polite, respectful, and I show intelligence and interest.

Homeless Woman slides over to the lunch table filled with lunch boxes.

She speaks directly to the camera.

> HOMELESS WOMAN
> I really don't get what people seem to have against vegetarian meals.

Homeless woman stares into the camera.

Nonchalant, she knocks several lunch boxes off the table into her conference bag.

INT. MOVIE SET – DAY

Homeless Woman fixes herself a plate of food.

>   HOMELESS WOMAN
>   Work as a television and movie extra
>   comes and goes, but craft services is
>   forever. (shrugging) They don't always
>   pay money but they always tell me to
>   eat!

EXT. UGLY BUILDING – DAY

The silhouette of a homeless person shows in a lighted window like Norman Bates' mother.

Homeless Woman stands in front of the building with a flip chart and pointer and speaks to the camera.

>   HOMELESS WOMAN
>   Okay. Why not the homeless shelter, you
>   ask. Well, I'll tell you. You've heard of
>   the Accidental Tourist, but are you at all
>   familiar with the Unintentional Zoo?

Homeless Woman points to images of bugs on the flip chart.

>   HOMELESS WOMAN
>   For instance... parasites? Scabies, lice,
>   fleas, ticks, roaches, bed bugs. It's like
>   an episode of Fear Factor where the
>   contestant lays in a glass coffin full of
>   earth worms or roaches for thousands of
>   dollars of prize money. Only... rather
>   than cash, the homeless person wins a
>   grand prize of encephalitis, malaria, or
>   Lyme disease.

Homeless Woman points to images of viruses on the flip chart.

                    HOMELESS WOMAN
          Then there's the viruses. You got your
          basic colds, your flus. Your hepatitis's.

Homeless Woman clicks through a power point presentation on tuberculosis.

                    HOMELESS WOMAN
          And here's our old friend, the bacteria.
          Shout out to tuberculosis! Holla! Or
          don't.

Homeless Woman clicks through a power point presentation on fungi.

                    HOMELESS WOMAN
          But to round out the exploration of the
          shelter's wild kingdom, let's throw in a
          little bit of fungi. A touch of athlete's
          foot in the showers.

Homeless Woman walks away from the homeless shelter.

                    HOMELESS WOMAN
          Rats? Mice? I just can't do it. I cannot
          pay the price of admission to the
          Unintentional Zoo. However, I will say
          this...

Homeless Woman stops walking.

                    HOMELESS WOMAN
          Parasites and vermin have nothing on
          the people. Let's take a closer look at
          what *people* bring to a homeless shelter,
          boys and girls.

Word crawl while Homeless Woman resumes walking away:

Thievery
Violence
Cursing
Drug/Alcohol abuse
Lack of Privacy
Rules
Paperwork
Jail-like atmosphere
Silencing
Religiosity
Exploitation
Humiliation
Disrespect
Condescension

EXT. EL TRAIN:PLATFORM – NIGHT

Homeless Woman stands under a heater and speaks to the camera.

> HOMELESS WOMAN
> Shall I go on? Really? Do you *really* want me to go on? Because I've seen and heard and *smelled* some things no human or animal was ever meant by God to see, hear, or smell. Things that I can't ever unsee, unhear, or unsmell.

INT. EL TRAIN:CAR – NIGHT

Homeless Woman sits in a seat with her suitcase and speaks to the camera.

HOMELESS WOMAN

Better the shelter than no place at all, some say. After all, beggars can't be choosers, some might explain further (shakes finger) shaking naughty fingers. *One week.* Seven days in a bed full of a menagerie of insects surrounded by a room full of human misery, disease, and desperation. On the eighth day, we'll check your physical, psychological, and emotional health. By the way, just how much of your health are you willing to gamble away in order to prove *that* point? Because I'll tell you right now...

EXT. UGLY BUILDING – DAY

HOMELESS WOMAN

The house always wins.

INT. EL TRAIN:PLATFORM – NIGHT

Homeless Woman stands underneath another heater and speaks to the camera.

HOMELESS WOMAN

So what to do? Well, after several forced death marches away from improvised, freelance shelters, the unhoused rely upon word-of-mouth, common sense, adaptability, creativity, anything, whatever it takes to survive. (pause) Or they die.

INT. O'HARE AIRPORT:LOBBY – NIGHT

                    HOMELESS WOMAN
Blend in at airports.

INT. GREYHOUND BUS STATION:LOBBY – DAY

                    HOMELESS WOMAN
Bus stations.

INT. AMTRAK/METRA TRAIN STATION:LOBBY - NIGHT

                    HOMELESS WOMAN
Train stations.

INT. MOVIE THEATER – NIGHT

                    HOMELESS WOMAN
Movie theatres.

INT. HOSPITAL:LOBBY – NIGHT

                    HOMELESS WOMAN
Hospitals.

INT. COLLEGE LIBRARY:STACKS – NIGHT

                    HOMELESS WOMAN
Universities and colleges.

INT. EL TRAIN:CAR – NIGHT

> HOMELESS WOMAN
> Ride like there's no tomorrow.

INT. LOWER WACKER – NIGHT

> HOMELESS WOMAN
> The boiler rooms keep it warm down here. But sometimes (coughing) it's still not enough.

INT. LONG HALLWAY – DAY

Homeless Woman's appearance is dusty and worn-down.

She walks the long hallway as if exhausted. She's coughing.

Her facial expression is twitchy when she looks into the camera.

> HOMELESS WOMAN
> Criminals and predators, law enforcement and security guards, exploitative religions and cults, business owners and housed residents, sickness, disease, malnutrition, and Mother Nature herself stalk after the vulnerable like hunters after game.

Homeless Woman's speech slurs.

Her steps slow.

                    HOMELESS WOMAN
     But   sometimes...   just   to   reach
     equilibrium,   sometimes...   Mother
     Nature evens the score.

Homeless Woman stops.

She blinks, twitches, and sways.

                    HOMELESS WOMAN
     Sometimes... the Deprived rise and
     return.

Homeless Woman now resembles a zombie.

Homeless Woman drools and moans and twitches.

Word crawl over Homeless Woman as she exhibits zombie-like
symptoms:

Symptoms of Sleep Deprivation include:
Irritability
Cognitive Impairment
Memory lapses or loss
Impaired moral judgment
Hallucinations
ADHD-like symptoms
Impaired immune system
Risk of diabetes 2
High blood pressure
Hypertension
Weight gain
Decreased reaction time
Confusion
Depression
Slurred speech
Lack of coordination and dexterity
Mania

Tremors and aches
Decreased body temperature
Paranoia

Symptoms of Malnutrition include:
Depression
Anxiety
Hallucinations
Headaches

Symptoms of Hypothermia include:
Low body temperature
Shivering
Stumbling
Confusion
Blue lips, ears, fingers and toes
Puffy skin
Difficulty in speaking
Amnesia
Incoherence
Irrational behavior
Stupor

Other Homeless Ills include:
Swollen feet
Cramped muscles
Extreme weather exposure
Lack of access to basic health and hygiene

> HOMELESS WOMAN
> (groaning, subtitled)
> Sleep deprivation is a psychological and physiological form of torture worse than hunger or thirst used against enemy combatants... and homeless citizens of the United States.

Title Card:

When there's no more room left in the homeless shelter, the unhoused will walk... to *your* home.

EXT. APT BUILDING - NIGHT

Homeless Woman shuffles towards the front entrance.

Homeless Woman coughs, groans, and sways on the porch.

Homeless Woman bangs on the windows with cans of change, shoes, and walking canes.

EXT. FAST FOOD RESTAURANT - NIGHT

A chorus of Homeless Extras groan.

EXT. APT BUILDING – NIGHT

Housed Resident, holding a sandwich, parts the curtains to look at Homeless Woman.

                    HOUSED RESIDENT
          You can't come in here. This is our
          home!

Housed Resident takes a big, spiteful bite out of the sandwich.

                    HOUSED RESIDENT
          Get a job!

EXT. FAST FOOD RESTAURANT - NIGHT

A chorus of Homeless Extras groan and drool on the window at the sight of piles of food on plates.

EXT. APT BUILDING - NIGHT

Homeless Woman rams shopping carts and luggage into the door.

EXT. FAST FOOD RESTAURANT - NIGHT

Homeless Extras pound on the windows.

EXT. HIGH-END HOTEL – NIGHT

Empty sofas, cushions, and area rugs fill an empty lobby.

There is a sound of breaking glass.

Homeless Extras overrun Security Guard.

EXT. FAST FOOD RESTAURANT - NIGHT

Homeless Extras rush towards piles of food.

INT. PUBLIC LIBRARY – NIGHT

Homeless Extras stagger through the stacks.

INT. APARTMENT BUILDING:APARTMENT – NIGHT

Homeless Woman enters the apartment of Housed Resident.

Housed Resident screams.

Homeless Woman rushes towards the table piled with food.

> HOUSED RESIDENT (shrieking)
> Get out of here!

Homeless Woman coughs and slobbers in the face of Housed Resident before she gnaws and snatches the sandwich out of the hands and mouth of Housed Resident.

Housed Resident screams in shock and disgust.

> HOUSED RESIDENT
> Nooooo!

Homeless Woman masticates greedily.

Housed Resident whimpers and cries from the floor, face smeared with food and saliva.

INT. HIGH-END HOTEL – NIGHT

Homeless Extras rush towards couches, area rugs, floors, beds to lay down.

INT. CLOSED SCHOOLS AND BUSINESSES – NIGHT

Homeless Extras sit at empty desks and fall asleep.

Homeless Extras lay on gymnasium floor and fall asleep.

INT. FAST FOOD RESTAURANT – NIGHT

Homeless Extras bathe in bathrooms.

INT. APARTMENT BUILDING:APARTMENT – NIGHT

Homeless Woman rolls around in the Housed Resident's king-size bed moaning and crying in relief.

Title Card:
We are legion.

FADE OUT
THE END

Storyboards

DEPRIVATION: THE APOCALYPSE

DEPRIVATION
THE APOCALYPSE

Storyboard Title Card

INT. TRAIN STATION : BATHROOM - NIGHT

Storyboard 1

INT TRAIN STATION. BATHROOM — NIGHT

Storyboard 2

Storyboard 3

Storyboard 4

INT. MOVIE THEATER - AUDITORIUM

Storyboard 5

INT. MOVIE THEATER - AUDITORIUM

Storyboard 6

Storyboard 7

Storyboard 8

Storyboard 9

104 LEE MCQUEEN

Storyboard 10

DEPRIVATION
THE APOCALYPSE

Storyboard End Card

BONUS Screenplay

DEEP IN THE WOODS

CAST OF CHARACTERS

The Woman – Black, female, mid 40s

The Man – mid 40s

TIME
Near future.

FADE IN

EXT. – CABIN – NIGHT

An iron fence surrounds an isolated cabin.

Light from a bonfire casts flickering shadows.

INT. - STONE CABIN - NIGHT

A baseball bat sits propped next to the front door.

A lit candle sits on a table.

A handwritten note demands:

"Give us the women or we kill everyone."

A sad-eyed WOMAN sits in a chair across from an angry MAN.

> WOMAN
> Do they want your mother too?

> MAN (snarling)
> What the hell do you think? She's seventy-five-years-old for God's sake.

> WOMAN (sarcastic)
> So just your wife and daughter. That's it?

> MAN
> Or they'll kill all of us.

WOMAN
We can't do that. I don't care about my
life as much as hers. She's too young to
have to face this.

MAN
So's our son.

WOMAN
She hasn't lived. She's our baby.

MAN
So's our son. He's lived less than anyone
of us.

WOMAN
I know. But it's wrong. You know what
they'll do to her. I'll do it. I'll go, but not
her. I'll go so she doesn't...

MAN
They want you both.

WOMAN
There *has* to be another way.

MAN
We've been through every option at least
forty different times the last forty days!
They'll starve us out. Burn us out. Or
shoot us out. We're surrounded and
outgunned.

WOMAN
Maybe we could just reason with them...

                    MAN
Reason? Reason with people wearing
the skins of the people who left us to go
for help? Rapists and cannibals? What
do you plan to say? Those *people* out
there are no longer human. It would be
easier to reason with one of those feral
dogs scavenging the city.

                    WOMAN
But...

The man slams his hands on the table.

                    MAN
But nothing! There's no one to help us.
Everybody we know is dead or turned
into those predators who drink blood
like water. Anything to survive. No one's
riding to the rescue. No police. No
national guard. No military. No nothing.
NOTHING!

                    WOMAN
Well, then what?

The man looks away.

                    WOMAN
What?!

The man shakes his head.

                    MAN
You know what has to happen.

                    WOMAN
It doesn't have to. We are still a family.
Not beasts like them.

                    MAN
Are you sure about that? After
civilization went back to the Stone Age,
we *all* became beasts.

                    WOMAN
We're not like them.

                    MAN
No. We don't hang human skeletons
from our fence. Yet. But who knows what
we'll do in a few months just to stay
alive. Maybe even weeks. Days.

                    WOMAN
Tonight?

                    MAN
WE'RE. OUT. OF. RESOURCES.

The woman sighs.

                    MAN
We don't have any food. We have two
days' worth of water. After that, we're
dead anyway and it won't matter.

The woman shakes her head.

                    MAN
They won't leave until they get what they
came for. (pause) At least this way...

                    WOMAN
What do you mean "at least this way?"

                    MAN
I can't fight them all. I can't protect you
or her.

                    WOMAN
No. Obviously, you can't.

The man stares at the woman for a long moment.

                    MAN
They're stronger. And there's more of
them.
                    WOMAN
Don't say it. I can't bear to hear that filth
come out of your mouth.

                    MAN
With them, you and she might live. You
have... a chance.

                    WOMAN
To become like them? To be their pets?
Slaves? How do you even know we'll
live? Maybe our skeletons will hang off
the hoods of their trucks and their
motorcycles too.

                    MAN
They want women. They want...

The woman makes a gagging sound.

                    MAN
They want... to breed. That means...

                    WOMAN (whispering)
          Please stop. Stop talking.

                    MAN
          We're out of options. There's no more
          ammunition. My mother's barely alive as
          it is. Our son's too young to fight and
          he's starving to death.

                    WOMAN
          So you'll trade us? Me and her? So *you*
          can live?

Long silence.

EXT. - STONE HOUSE – NIGHT

Shadowy silhouettes surround the house.
Bonfires create more shadows.

Chanting.

Drums beat louder.

INT. STONE HOUSE – NIGHT

                    WOMAN
          I thought I understood this world. I
          thought I understood *you*. But I didn't
          understand a single thing.

                    MAN
          Would you rather we all died?

The woman sobs.

                    WOMAN
You know that I don't.

                    MAN
Since you can't decide, maybe we should
ask her what *she* would do to save her
younger brother's life.

                    WOMAN
And yours?

Long silence.

                    WOMAN (disgusted)
Even wild dogs care for their young.

Too angry to speak, the man stands, knocking his chair over.

He turns his back and walks away to a peep hole.

He looks outside.

The silhouettes still surround the house.

The drums beat louder.

EXT. STONE HOUSE - NIGHT

The people surrounding the house chant even louder.

INT. STONE HOUSE – NIGHT

                    MAN (quietly)
She's dying anyway.

                    WOMAN
But we don't have to kill her.

                    MAN
          Or you?

Silence.

The woman shakes her head.

                    WOMAN
          Don't you do that. You are in *no* position
          to judge me.

                    MAN
          We can't get any more antivirals with
          those monsters out there. How much
          longer do you think she'll last?

                    WOMAN
          You've become a cruel man. Or maybe
          you always were.

                    MAN (shouting)
          And maybe *you* can't face the reality of a
          cruel world! She's getting sicker! If we
          send her out there...

                    WOMAN
          If *you* send US out there. Like you said...

                    MAN
          Like *they* said.

The man paces back-and-forth.

                    MAN
          If they acquire the virus and pass it
          around among themselves, then they die
          too.

The woman cries again.

> WOMAN
> They'll pass *her* around. And me too.

> MAN
> It's the ONLY WAY!

> WOMAN
> God help us. Please. If You even exist anymore, please help us.

Running feet.

A door slams.

The woman and man run to the front door which is wide open. The woman screams.

> WOMAN
> She's gone! Oh my God. She heard you. She ran out there to them!

The man stands in the doorway, undecided.

> WOMAN (shrieking)
> Do something!

The man doesn't move.

The chanting stops.

A roar goes up from the darkness.

The woman runs out of the front door wailing.

> WOMAN
> Noooo! Don't hurt her!

The man lifts his arm to stop her. Then he drops his arm to his side.

He bows his head.

More roars from the crowd.

When the screaming of his wife and daughter starts, the man closes the front door, locks it, and sinks to the floor sobbing.

He grabs the baseball bat by the door.

He screams and yells and wrecks the room.

EXT. STONE HOUSE – DAWN

Engines roar in the distance.

Burnt out fires, bloody clothing, pieces of flesh, and trash surround the steel gate.

Bones hang from the steel gate.

INT. STONE HOUSE – DAWN

The table and a chair are broken on the floor.

The candle is smashed on the floor.

The bloody baseball bat lays on the floor in the center of the room.

Beside the baseball bat the other chair lays on its side.

Above the chair, the man swings from a noose.

FADE OUT
THE END

BONUS Storyboards

DEEP IN THE WOODS

Storyboard Title Card

Storyboard Quotation

Storyboard 1

Storyboard 2

Storyboard 3

EXT CABIN NIGHT

STILL SHOT   Firelight. Male clarb Drumbers.

Storyboard 4

EXT CABIN NIGHT

STILL SHOT   Firelight. Male clarb Drumbers.   Nitrous
                                                  roll.

Storyboard 5

Storyboard 5.1

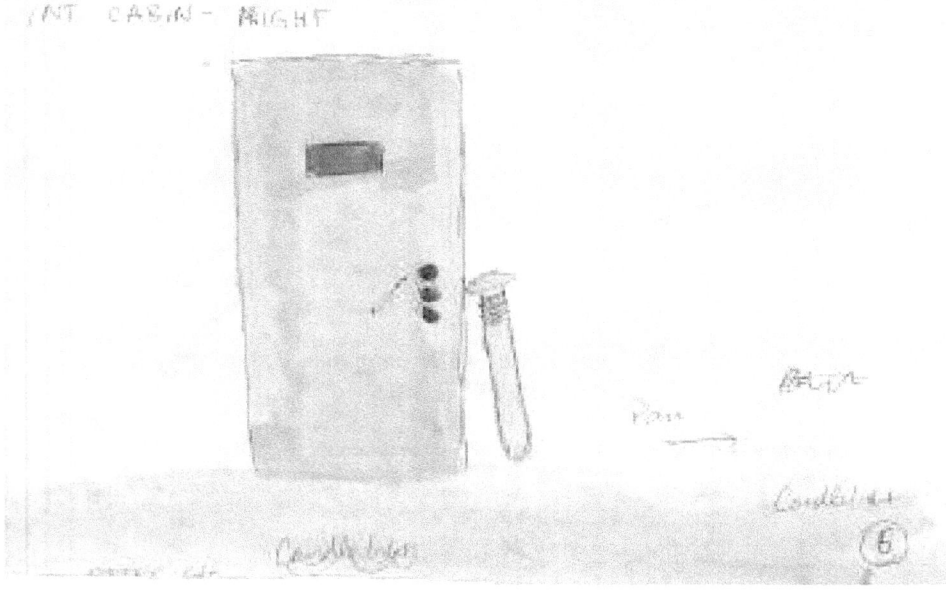

Storyboard 6

Storyboard 7

Storyboard 8

124 LEE MCQUEEN

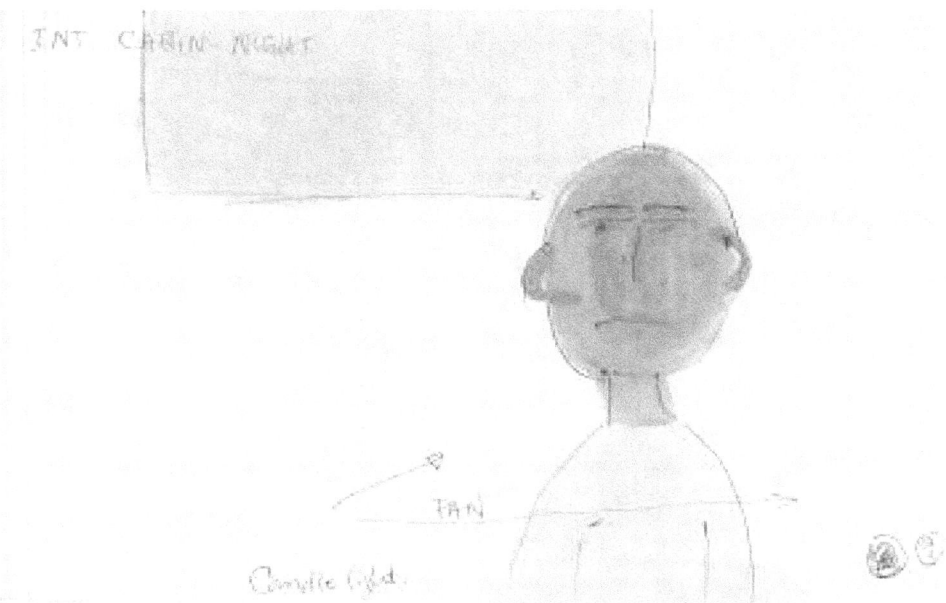

Storyboard 9

Storyboard 10

Storyboard 11

Storyboard 12

Storyboard 13

Storyboard 14

Storyboard 15

Storyboard 16

Storyboard 17

Storyboard 18

Storyboard 19

Storyboard 20

Storyboard 21

Storyboard 23

Storyboard 23.1

Storyboard 24

Storyboard 26

Storyboard 28

Storyboard 29

Storyboard 29.1

Storyboard 30

Storyboard 30.2

Storyboard 31

Storyboard 32

Storyboard 32.1

Storyboard 33

Storyboard 34

Storyboard 35

Storyboard 36

Storyboard 36.1

Storyboard 37

Storyboard 38

Storyboard 39

Storyboard 40

Storyboard 42

Storyboard 43

Storyboard 44

Storyboard 45

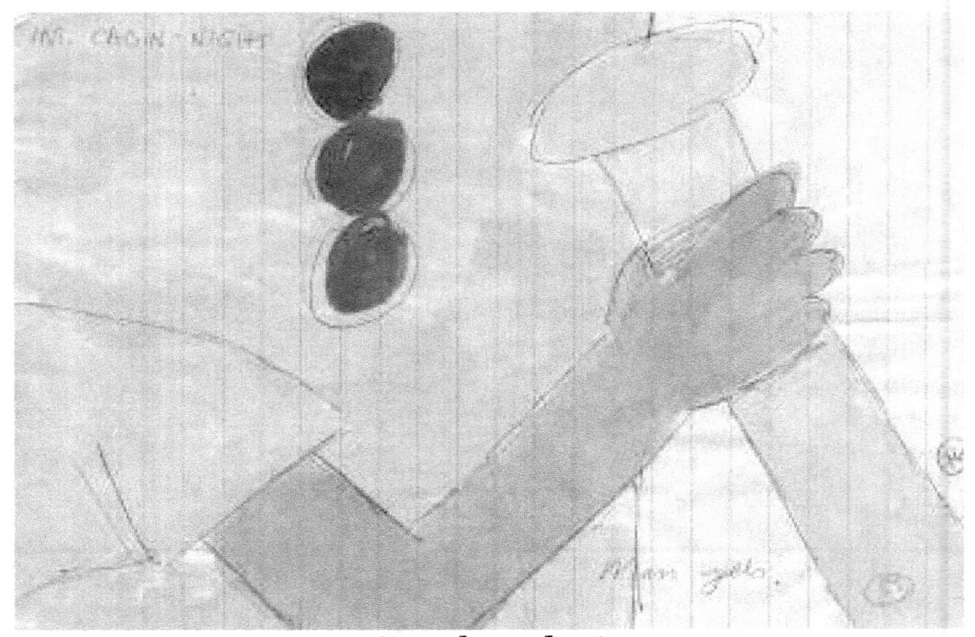

Storyboard 46

Storyboard 47

Storyboard 48

Storyboard 49

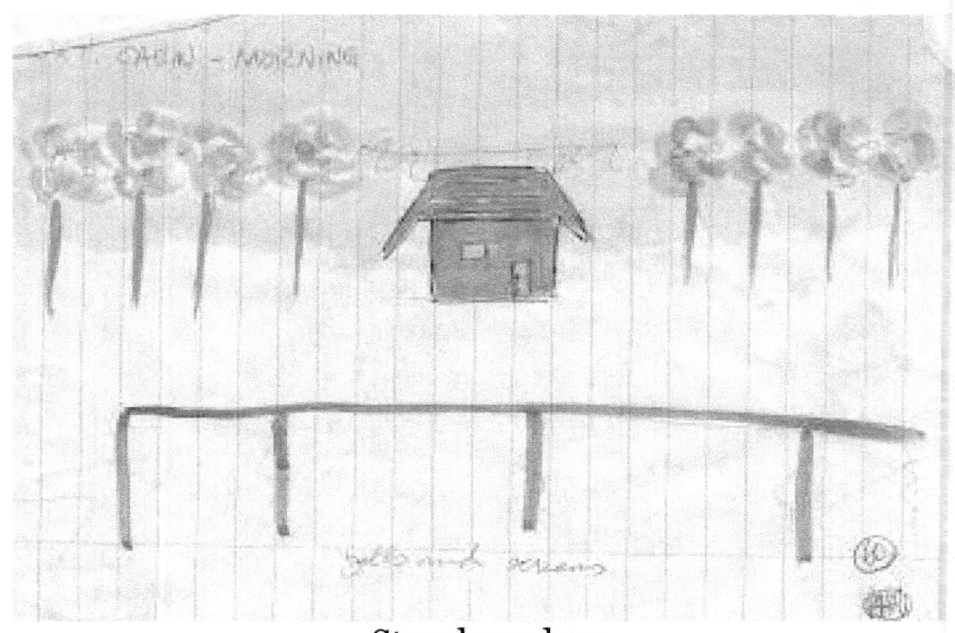

Storyboard 50

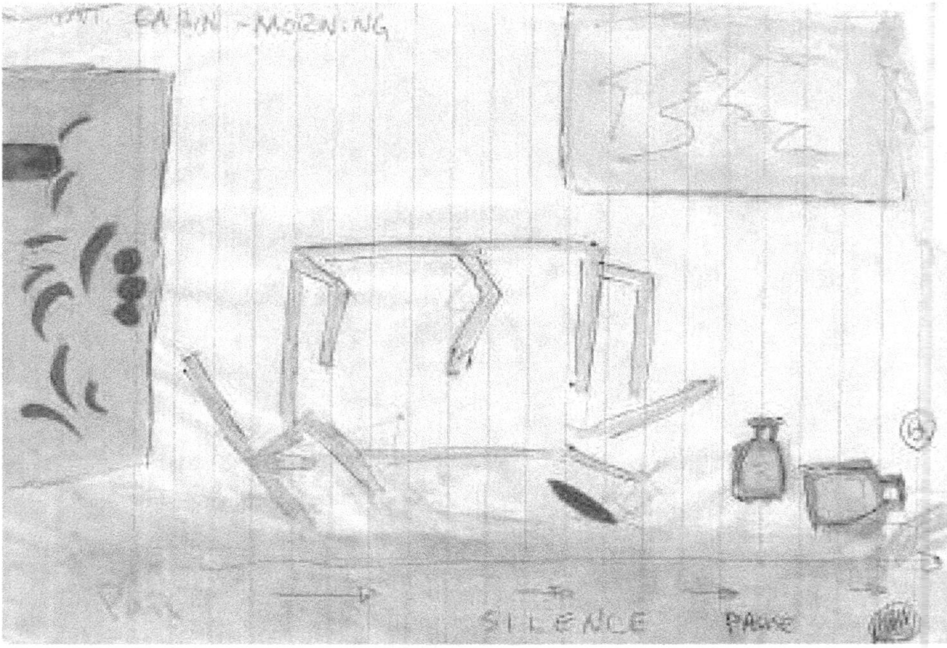

Storyboard 51

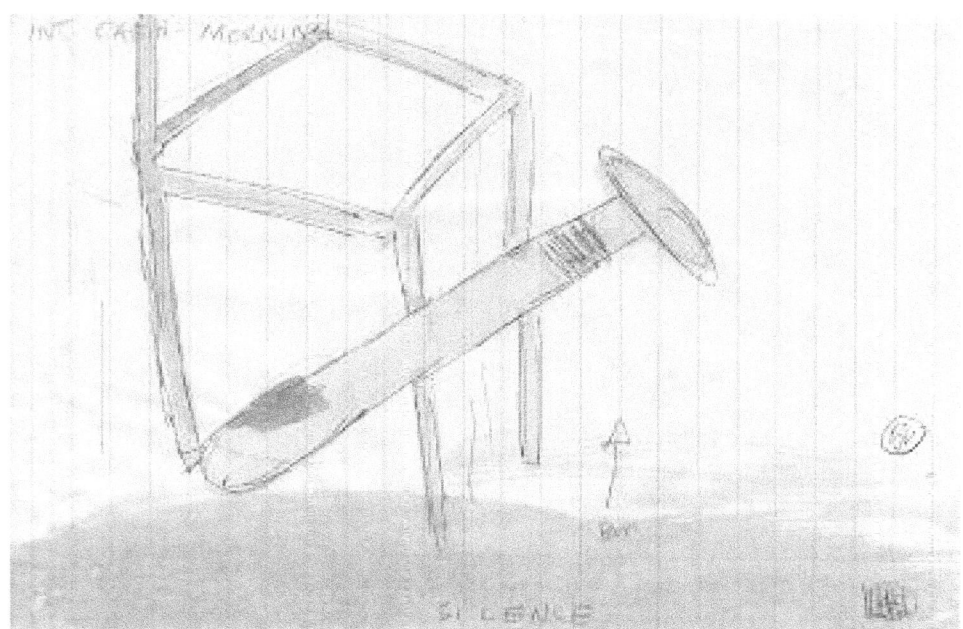

Storyboard 52

Storyboard 53

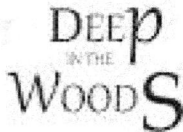

Storyboard End Card

ABOUT THE AUTHOR

Lee McQueen enjoys writing, research, water colors, gardening, and traveling. She has been a librarian, a bookstore owner, and a substitute teacher and holds an MLS from SUNY-Buffalo, a BA from Xavier University, and coursework in public affairs at the University of Texas at Austin. Now editor and publisher at McQueen Press, her projects include novels, poetry, short stories, screenplays, and greeting cards.

AUTHOR'S NOTE

Homelessness, deprivation, isolation, and the extreme mental and emotional stress that results is a clear indication of the harm caused to the greater community by severe wealth inequality.

Wealth inequality is unrestrained, unregulated, rapacious capitalism taken to such an extreme that it causes regular society to suffocate, decline, and and then to die under the sheer weight of vulgar, classless, godless greed.

Godless, because believers have always understood that citizens of a nation who answer to God also obey the command to render unto Caesar, that which is Caesar's... and then do so. While apparently the godless and greedy refuse to render their fair share to Caesar, meaning that it is the citizens and believers, who despite their poverty, are required to make up the difference to keep the nation functional.

And so wealth transfers from the citizens to the elite.

No other group of what some may generously call humans, have quite matched the unique achievements of these godless and greedy people.

Truly, the elite will ever be remembered and never be forgotten for their use of ill-gotten gains as false philanthropy and fake charity wielded like weapons for societal control mechanisms which have degraded the quality of life for the citizens upon which they sit as over-sized gorillas.

ACKNOWLEDGMENTS

Thank you to the greedy disaster capitalists around the world who have shown themselves willing to lie, cheat, steal, kill, and destroy everything and everyone on Planet Earth for the sheer psychopathic joy of acquiring more resources, money, power, and control.

The Bezos, The Gates, The Zuckerbergs, The Musks, The Buffets, The Ellisons, The Waltons, The Bloombergs, The Kochs, are to be commended for their tireless efforts to serve as examples to the entire world of how to be ugly and disgusting. How to take from the poor and take from the poor and take from the poor, and then to use what they take from the poor as the very means to devour the poor.

Without you, these screenplays would have no point or purpose.

THE MOUNTAINS REACH

Up to heaven, to the stars
To the universe
To join with God
To sing with the angels
We send our greetings to the world
We lift our Earth as a gift
To those who come to see
Our offerings
And hear
Our prayers
And not
Pass us by

Suspense Novel
ISBN 13 978-1533068194
ISBN 10 1533068194
2016
Stephanie Madison, a pariah to her family, launches a successful suicide attack against her employer, Cadis Industries. Though Stephanie dies in the attack, the strange menace that stalked Stephanie's life now targets her niece, Marietta Brazil. Forced to flee her city of birth as well as her adopted home, Marietta finally draws a line in the sand to confront the corrupt forces that destroyed her family. But though she fights the evil outside, can she truly face the darkness within?

Short Screenplay Collection

ISBN-13: 978-0-9798515-5-1

2013

These screen-ready tales of dark fantasy, horror, and adventure reflect possible rather than impossible worlds. Great stories for lovers of afro-futurism and speculative fiction. Plenty of monologues and dialogues for drama students and teachers, actors, screenwriters, producers, and directors.

Travel Memoir
ISBN-13: 978-0979851568
2013
In 2012, Lee McQueen traveled from Colorado through Kansas, Oklahoma, Arkansas, Tennessee, Mississippi, Alabama, Georgia, Missouri, Illinois, Iowa, Nebraska, and then back to Colorado to promote her latest romance novel. From Beale Street to Route 66 to the Great River Road, to Colfax Avenue--in the spirit of Jack Kerouac and Johnny Appleseed--she fell in love with the road. This collection of journal entries, blog postings, narration in retrospect, and watercolors reveals surprises on Lee's journey through Middle America.

Suspense/Romance Novel
ISBN-13: 978-0979851575
2012
A cross-country chase carries Tolly Henry and Scott Windrunner on an adventure from Midwestern rolling prairies to southwestern Rocky Mountains. Roadside motels, truck stops, corn silos, and windmills guide Scott's whirlwind rundown of Tolly amid echoes of past military service, domestic violence, and post-traumatic stress.

Action/Adventure Screenplay
ISBN-13:978-0979851599
2nd ed.

2011

On a Christian mission to redeem slaves in Sudan, a reformed female gang member Davey is kidnapped and sold into slavery herself. She uses her former street experiences and talent for leadership to convince the other slaves to break free and flee to the Ethiopian border. Everything Davey has ever learned will save her life.

Suspense/Drama Novel
ISBN-13: 978-0979851582
2010

As *Dallas* and *Dynasty* showcased the wealth, sex, intrigue, and power that drove the oil industry, so *Celara Sun* reveals the tumultuous world behind solar and wind. Martina Butler matches Alexander King step-for-step in a battle of wills to control Lake City's solar and wind energy markets. During the green revolution, the players realize that life moves forward, never backward—and it certainly doesn't stand still.

Non-fiction/Reference
ISBN-13: 978-0979851544
2008
This non-fiction reference work collects the interviews and submissions of fiction and non-fiction writers who discuss the impact of libraries on their career development. Numerous transcripts, photos, biographies, library quotations, footnotes, a glossary, and an index present the information as a teaching tool for the reader.

Romance/Family Drama Novel
ISBN-13: 978-0979851520
2007
Kenzi, an intelligent, sensitive woman living in small-town Texas, feels alienated from the person she knows she should be and would be if only she truly believed it possible. If Kenzi finds the ability to forgive her own mistakes and the mistakes of others, she may have a chance to meet her destiny head-on.

Poetry Collection
ISBN 978-0-978515-3-7
2007
2nded.
Out of Print
Poems speak on uncertainty, sadness, despair, guilt, anger, frustration, love, hope, forgiveness, happiness, joy, and spirituality. Poetry is interactive. The reader or listener meets the author or speaker halfway and fills the poem with their own reality and expectations. A lot like life and diamonds, poetry reflects back an image that depends on where one stands in relation to the expressions.

Short Story Collection
ISBN-13: 978-0979851506
2006
Fourteen short stories describe inner turmoil that drives change. Especially when the characters who inhabit the stories step outside the ordinary for a moment in time. And so, there remains the Imaginarium, where Dreamers know when to take a chance and Heroes know when to make a stand. Because refusing to make a choice is a choice. And sometimes, the least of all has the greatest ability to influence the future of the world.

www.ingramcontent.com/pod-product-compliance
Lightning Source LLC
Chambersburg PA
CBHW070550180626
46817CB00005B/1772